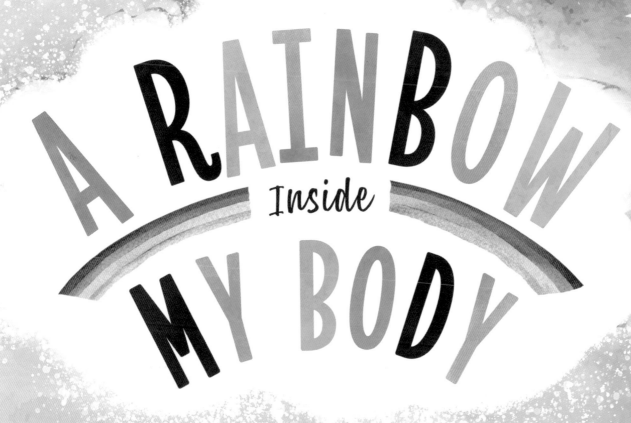

A RAINBOW Inside MY BODY

Finding Peace Through Yoga, Breathing Exercises, and the Chakras

WRITTEN BY
E. KATHERINE KOTTARAS
AND VANITHA SWAMINATHAN

ILLUSTRATED BY
HOLLY HATAM

VIKING

Sahasrāra = Suh-hus-raa-ruh (crown chakra)

Ājñā = Aaj-nyaa (third eye chakra)

Viśuddha = Vi-shu-ddha (throat chakra)

Anāhata = Uh-naa-huh-tuh (heart chakra)

Maṇipūra = Muh-ni-poor-uh (solar plexus chakra)

Svādhiṣṭhāna = Svaa-dhisht-haa-nuh (sacral chakra)

Mūlādhāra = Moo-lah-dhaa-ruh (root chakra)

A rainbow inside my body
twirls
and whirls
and spins.

Inside, chakras
keep me dancing,
like raindrops
in the sun.

Like the light, my body changes—
my mind shifts somewhat, too.

And when I need to know how I am feeling,
I can close my eyes and breathe.

A tree inside my body
grows with roots
that dig down deep.

Though wild winds push
and heavy storms pound—

I have this,
my first, red chakra,
both feet and each firm leg.

I am anchored,
safe and strong.

And when I need to feel grounded,
I can close my eyes and breathe.

A river inside my body
craves a clear and open path.

Though twigs fall in
and stones block waves—

I have this,
my second, orange chakra,
my sacrum and my hips.

I feel creative,
happy, and free.

And when I need inspiration,
I can close my eyes and breathe.

A sun inside my body
shines a warm and glowing light.

Though dark clouds roll
and shadows fall—

I have this,
my third, yellow chakra,
my stomach and my back.

I am powerful
and strong.

And when I need confidence,
I can close my eyes and breathe.

A flower inside my body
blooms with a soft and gentle scent.

Though mud may splash
and petals wither—

I have this,
my fourth, green chakra,
with my heart,
both arms, and hands.

I spread love, beauty,
and kindness.

And when I need gentle healing,
I can close my eyes and breathe.

A breeze inside my body
blows a calm and honest song.

Though thunder rumbles
over the land—

I have this,
my fifth, blue chakra,
my mouth
and each true word.

I speak my heart
and share my thoughts.

And when I need rhythm to sing my song,
I can close my eyes and breathe.

A bird inside my body
flies with focus
and with grace.

Though its wings
may tremble
and steer it astray—

I have this,
my sixth, indigo chakra,
my third eye
above my brow.

I see clearly
with much wisdom.

And when I need a new direction,
I can close my eyes and breathe.

The night sky inside my body
wraps and holds me tight.

Though the sun has
gone to sleep
for now—

I have this,
my seventh, white chakra,
the crown of my head
connecting to
each twinkling star.

I understand
and am at peace.

And when I need to feel comfort,
I can close my eyes and breathe.

There is a world inside my body.

I am one with everything.

The seven chakras
help the energy flow,
from the top of my head
down to each tiny toe.

I am nature,
and nature is me.

And when I need to feel anything,
I can close my eyes and breathe.

AUTHORS' NOTE

WHAT ARE THE CHAKRAS?

One part of yoga talks about how the body is organized into seven major power centers, called chakras, that work together. These chakras are often described as round spoked wheels, like pools of spiraling energy that exist inside our bodies and that have an impact on our minds.

Chakra = Cakra (Wheel)

Sahasrāra = Suh-hus-raa-ruh (crown chakra)

Ājñā = Aaj-nyaa (third eye chakra)

Viśuddha = Vi-shu-ddha (throat chakra)
Anāhata = Uh-naa-huh-tuh (heart chakra)
Maṇipūra = Muh-ni-poor-uh (solar plexus chakra)
Svādhiṣṭhāna = Svaa-dhisht-haa-nuh (sacral chakra)
Mūlādhāra = Moo-lah-dhaa-ruh (root chakra)

By becoming aware of these pools of energy, we will be able to balance our emotions and, as a result, bring balance into our lives. If we feel this harmony in our bodies, minds, and spirits, we will be able to make better decisions and learn how to respond to stress healthfully.

WHAT IS YOGA?

Yoga is a philosophy going back five thousand years to ancient India. In addition to the poses, the ancient writings of the Yoga Sutras, written by a sage named Patanjali, offer ways we can become more comfortable in our bodies and settle any stress that we might struggle with inside our minds. The word "yoga," which comes from Sanskrit, the ancient Indian language, translates literally as "to yoke" or "to unite." When we practice yoga, we are trying to unite the different parts of our being—our changing bodies, our constantly thinking minds, our deep sense of self, our relationships with others—so that we can move through the world with a greater sense of calm and peace.

WHAT IS AYURVEDA?

Ayurveda is the world's oldest holistic ("all encompassing" or "whole") healing system, which is a sister science of yoga. Ayurveda comes from two Sanskrit words: "ayur," meaning life, and "veda," meaning knowledge or science. It was also developed in India more than three thousand years ago. It is a traditional system of medicine that helps the body, mind, and spirit by paying attention to food, herbs, movement, meditation, and breathing. By breathing in specific ways and by eating certain foods that align with the chakras, we can help our bodies feel balanced on the inside as well.

THE BREATH INSIDE MY BODY

INTRODUCTION TO CHAKRAS — *RAINBOW BREATH*

Stand tall with both feet firm on the ground. Take a deep breath in, lifting your arms above your head, and as you exhale, dip to one side like the arc of a rainbow. As you inhale, come back up to center. As you exhale again, dip to the other side.

THE FIRST CHAKRA: ROOT — *TREE BREATH*

Stand tall with both feet firm on the ground, hands on your heart. Bring to mind a tall tree. Close your eyes and imagine the base of the tree's trunk, right where the roots start to dig into the earth. As you inhale, allow your breath to follow the length of the trunk all the way up past the limbs and branches to the very top of the tree. As you exhale, allow your breath to follow the length of the tree down, all the way past the branches and limbs, down toward the roots, where you can release the breath.

THE SECOND CHAKRA: SACRAL — *OCEAN BREATH*

Bring to mind a calm summer beach, with the sound of the waves as they move to shore and then back into the deep. Take a breath in, and as you exhale, make the sound "haaaa," so you sound like the waves, too.

THE THIRD CHAKRA: SOLAR PLEXUS — *CANDLE BREATH*

Sit comfortably, lift one hand close to your lips, breathe in through the nose, and blow out the air softly on the tip of each finger, as though they are candles, feeling the light within your belly.

THE FOURTH CHAKRA: HEART — *LOVING BREATH*

Lie down and place your favorite stuffed animal on your belly. Take a deep breath in to lift your belly and give your loved animal a gentle ride in the air. Exhale so that it will come back down softly. Imagine how happy it must feel having you offer this kind gift.

THE FIFTH CHAKRA: THROAT — *HUMMING BREATH*

Sit comfortably, take a deep breath in, and as you exhale, hum with the sound "mmmm." If it's comfortable, place a finger gently over each ear and notice the difference in the sound as you breathe out.

THE SIXTH CHAKRA: THIRD EYE — *PINWHEEL BREATH*

Sit comfortably with your eyes open or closed. Inhale, and then as you exhale, look to the left. Inhale and focus your eyes back to center, then as you exhale, look up. Inhale and focus your eyes back to center, and exhale as you look to the right. Inhale and focus your eyes back to center, and exhale as you look down. Inhale and focus your eyes back to center, and then go in the opposite direction (moving your eyes right, down, left, then up). Then, with eyes closed and still, take three deep breaths.

THE SEVENTH CHAKRA: CROWN — *LION'S BREATH*

Sit comfortably, take a deep breath in, and as you exhale, send your gaze to the sky, stick out your tongue, and let out a big "*haaaaa!*"

THE FULL WHEEL — *COLOR BREATH*

Sit comfortably, close your eyes, and as you breathe in, bring to mind the color red, then as you breathe out, bring to mind the color orange. Breathe in the color yellow; breathe out green. Breathe in blue; breathe out indigo. Breathe in white, and breathe out white.

Breathe in again, imagining the full spectrum of light blending and dancing together inside your body and throughout the skies above.

A BERRY INSIDE MY BODY

INTRODUCTION TO CHAKRAS: THE RAINBOW

When we eat certain foods in line with the chakras, it increases energy and creates balance in the mind and the body.

THE FIRST CHAKRA: ROOT
(ELEMENT—EARTH)

Vegetables: Carrot, potato, radish, beet

Fruits: Red apple, watermelon, pomegranate, berries

THE SECOND CHAKRA: SACRAL
(ELEMENT—WATER)

Vegetables: Carrot, squash, pepper

Fruits: Melon, mango, tangerine, orange

THE THIRD CHAKRA: SOLAR PLEXUS
(ELEMENT—FIRE)

Vegetables: Yellow pepper, corn

Fruits: Banana, lemon

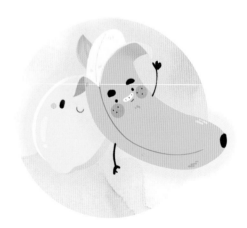

THE FOURTH CHAKRA: HEART
(ELEMENT—AIR)

Vegetables: Kale, lettuce, spinach, broccoli

Fruits: Green apple, avocado

THE FIFTH CHAKRA: THROAT
(ELEMENT—SOUND)

Vegetables: Seaweed

Fruits: Blueberry, peach, pear, apricot, plum

THE SIXTH CHAKRA: THIRD EYE
(ELEMENT—LIGHT)

Vegetables: Eggplant, purple potato

Fruits: Goji berry, acai, Concord grape, blackberry

THE SEVENTH CHAKRA: CROWN
(ELEMENT—SPACE)

Vegetables: Cucumber, squash, cabbage

Fruits: Any fruit

THE FULL WHEEL

In order to grow, we need nutritious food, water, fresh air, and sunlight.

VIKING
An imprint of Penguin Random House LLC, New York

First published in the United States of America by Viking, an imprint of Penguin Random House LLC, 2024

Text copyright © 2024 by E. Katherine Kottaras and Vanitha Swaminathan
Illustrations copyright © 2024 by Holly Hatam

Visit us online at PenguinRandomHouse.com.

Library of Congress Cataloging-in-Publication Data is available.

ISBN 9780593465691
1 3 5 7 9 10 8 6 4 2

Manufactured in China

TOPL

Edited by Tamar Brazis
Design by Lily K. Qian
Text set in Emy Slab

FOR ROHAN, SHAAN, NOAH, NINA, ARI, AND AYLA —V. S.

FOR OLLY —E. K. K.

DEDICATED TO LITTLE EXPLORERS, FINDING MAGIC IN
EVERY BREATH, AND COLOR IN EVERY MOVE. —H. H.